The Magic Goose

D0438965

The Magic Goose

by **DANIEL PINKWATER**

illustrated by
JILL PINKWATER

A
LITTLE APPLE
PAPERBACK

SCHOLASTIC INC.
New York   Toronto   London   Auckland   Sydney

If you purchased this book without a cover, you should be aware that this book is stolen property. It was reported as "unsold and destroyed" to the publisher, and neither the author not the publisher has received any payment for this "stripped book."

No part of this publication may be reproduced in whole or in part, or stored in a retrieval system, or transmitted in any form or by any means, electronic, mechanical, photocopying, recording, or otherwise, without written permission of the publisher. For information regarding permission, write to Scholastic, Inc., Attention: Permissions Department, 555 Broadway, New York, NY 10012.

ISBN 0-590-31349-5

Text copyright © 1997 by Daniel Pinkwater.
Illustrations copyright © 1997 by Jill Pinkwater.
All rights reserved. Published by Scholastic Inc.
LITTLE APPLE PAPERBACKS and logos are trademarks of Scholastic Inc.

12 11 10 9 8 7 6 5 4 3 2 1   7 8 9/9 0 1 2/0

Printed in the U.S.A.
First Scholastic printing, October 1997

To Geese and other creatures of goodwill.
                                    — DP & JP

Contents

The Magic Goose

1
Seymour

My name is Seymour Semolina, and I like to read. I read a lot. Twice a year, when my mother, Selma Semolina, and my father, Steven Semolina, go to parents' night at school, my teacher, Mrs. Mulberry, tells them, "Seymour is a good reader."

I not only read books in school, I read books on the bus, going to school and going home. I read comics and magazines. I read most of the newspaper every day. When I eat my breakfast, I read the cereal box. I read while listening to the radio. I read while watching TV. I read in the bathroom. When I ride in the family car, I read in the backseat. Sometimes I read two things at once. When I play baseball, I read while waiting for my turn at bat. Sometimes, I read while playing left field. I can also read while riding my bicycle, but my father made me promise not to, for fear of accidents. I am a reading fiend.

Saturdays, I go to the library. I read a book there — maybe two books. I usually check out five books and take them home.

Every night I read in bed. When my mother makes me turn out the light, I read under the covers with a flashlight.

I have two favorite books. One is *The Haphazard House Junior Dictionary for Little Scholars.* The other is *Seymour and the Magic Pudding* by my favorite author, Nathaniel Inkblotter. I like that book because it is about a kid named Seymour, just like me.

In *Seymour and the Magic Pudding,* this kid, Seymour, is in bed at night. He notices that something is in the room. He's pretty sure it is a monster.

The monster says, "Are you scared?"

Seymour says, "No. I am not scared."

The kids in stories like this are never scared.

The monster turns out to be a magic thing. It looks like a big pile of tapioca

pudding, It says, "I have come to visit you. I will be your friend."

Then Seymour and the magic pudding go out the window. Seymour's parents do not wake up while all this is happening. They don't have a clue.

Seymour and the magic pudding have an adventure. They fly through the air. They visit strange lands. They dance and play. In books like this, the kid always learns a lesson. Maybe it's about how wonderful imagining things can be, or about how you should never be scared. In *Seymour and the Magic Pudding,* Seymour learns that tapioca is your friend.

Then the magic pudding brings him home. He winds up back in his bed.

"Will you ever come back?" Seymour asks the magic pudding.

"Yes, I will come back," the magic pudding says. "I will be your friend. Now go to sleep."

And Seymour goes to sleep.

It's a heck of a book.

I wouldn't mind if something like that happened to me.

2
Magic

My other favorite book, *The Haphazard House Junior Dictionary for Little Scholars,* is a killer. It's got everything. I read it every night.

On this particular night, I was reading about fowl.

> **fowl** *foul*\ **1:** a bird of any kind **2a:** a domestic cock or hen; *esp*: an adult hen **b:** any of several domesticated or wild gallinaceous birds **3:** the meat of fowl used as food

Fascinating. Next, I looked up "gallina-ceous," because that was a word I did not know.

> **gallinaceous** *gal-in-ay-shus*\: of or relating to an order *(Galliformes)* of heavy-bodied largely terrestrial birds, including the pheasants, turkeys, grouse, and the common domestic fowl

Then, I had to look up "terrestrial." I almost knew what that meant, because I knew that an extraterrestrial is a being from outer space. It turned out that terrestrial means living on land or the earth.

You can't beat *The Haphazard House Junior Dictionary for Little Scholars.* I wonder what sort of book Nathaniel Inkblotter would write if he had a copy.

After I had read for as long as I could, when I felt my eyes closing, I switched off the light, rolled over, and went to sleep.

One moment I was sleeping, and the next moment I was awake. At first, I thought I might be dreaming I was awake. I wiggled around. I was pretty sure I was awake. I kept my eyes shut. I could not remember waking up like this, in the dark. It was an odd feeling.

Plus, I had an odd feeling on top of the odd feeling. I felt a tingling all over my skin. My nose kept wrinkling, all by itself, as though it were trying to smell something — but at first there was nothing to smell. Then I thought I smelled a smell like the smell of my Uncle Dave. Uncle Dave smokes cheap cigars.

Something's up, I thought.

I opened one eye.

I opened the other eye.

Something is in this room, I thought.

I sat up. "Who's there?"

"Me. I'm here."

"Who said that?" I said.

"I did."

I looked around the room. I saw something pale and gray. It was in the corner. It was dim, and hard to see — but it was there. Something was certainly there.

"Are you a ghost?" I asked.

"Would you be scared if I were?" the dim gray thing asked.

"I'm not scared," I said.

"I'm not a ghost."

"Are you something magic?" I asked.

"I sure am," the gray thing said.

"I'm turning on the light," I said.

"Go right ahead."

I turned on the light.

"You're a goose!" I said.

"I am. You have a problem with that?"

It was a very large goose, larger than any goose I had ever heard of or imagined. This goose was larger than a large person. I was not sure whether I had actually ever seen a live goose before — but I'd seen pictures of geese, and a goose is what this was. In the light the goose was a beautiful gray. Its beak was orange. It smelled of cheap cigars.

"You aren't a magic goose, by any chance?" I asked.

"A magic goose. Yes, indeed I am!" the goose said.

"This is good," I said. "What magic can you do? What kind of special powers do you have?"

"I can speak English."

"Excellent!" I said. "What else?"

"What else? What do you mean, 'what else?' You know any other geese who can talk?"

"I don't know any geese at all," I said.

"Well, if you had any experience with geese, you'd know that a talking one is fairly spectacular."

"I agree," I said. "But how about other magic powers? For example, can you take me flying? Can we visit strange lands? Can we dance and sing? Will I learn a lesson?"

"I have no idea what you are talking about," said the goose.

"You haven't?" I asked.

"Nope."

"But you are a magic goose," I said.

"I am."

"So, what magic can you do?"

"I got into your room. I'm talking to you. Forget about geese — are you aware of any animals of any kind who can do that?"

"Well, no," I agreed.

"See? Magic."

"In stories, like *Seymour and the Magic Pudding,* for example, they go someplace."

"Who does?"

"The kid and the magic thing," I said.

"Oh."

"Aren't we going someplace?" I asked.

"We will go to the kitchen."

"The kitchen?"

"Yes," the goose said.

3
In the
Kitchen

The magic goose and I went to the kitchen. Just like in *Seymour and the Magic Pudding*, my mother, Selma Semolina, and my father, Steven Semolina, did not wake up.

When we got to the kitchen, I turned on the light. The goose looked around.

"Nice kitchen," the goose said.

"Now what?" I asked.

"Let's make soup," the goose said.

"Goose soup?"

"Ha, ha. Very funny. We will make corn-flakes soup."

"Cornflakes soup?"

"Yes," the magic goose said.

"How do you make that?"

"You put cornflakes in a bowl. Then you pour milk. Then you put sugar on. Then you eat it."

"That's not cornflakes soup! That's cornflakes."

"It's wet. You eat it with a spoon. You eat it out of a bowl. I call that soup. If you ate

them dry, out of the box, then you could say cornflakes."

"That makes sense, I suppose," I said.

"See? You learned something," the goose said.

"This isn't as good as in the book," I said.

"Look, you are talking with a goose," the goose said. "A goose who speaks English — a magic goose. I came to your room. I came in the night. I taught you the difference between cornflakes and cornflakes soup — and we're going to make some. So stop complaining."

"I'm sorry."

"It's all right," the goose said. "Help me with the milk."

I fixed some cornflakes soup for the goose.

I fixed some for myself.

We sat at the table and ate our cornflakes soup.

"That was good," the goose said.

"Now what?" I asked.

"What do you mean, 'now what?'" the goose asked.

"I mean, what happens now?" I said.

The goose thought. "We could have some more cornflakes soup. You want some more cornflakes soup?"

"No," I said. "I'm full."

The magic goose and I sat and looked at each other across the table. Neither of us said anything for a while.

"Do you want some more cornflakes soup?" I asked the goose.

"Not really," the goose said.

We sat in silence. The goose looked around at the kitchen. I looked at the goose.

"Isn't this fun?" the goose asked.

"I was just thinking," I said. "Aside from the fact that you are a magic goose, it is sort of boring."

"I don't know how you can say that," the goose said. "We're practically having a party here."

"You've never done this before, have you?" I asked.

"Done what?"

"The magic goose thing — coming into a kid's room in the middle of the night — you've never done it before, am I right?"

"Well, not as such," the goose said. "But I'd say I'm doing an excellent job."

"You've never read any of the books about this sort of thing, have you?" I asked.

"Actually, geese don't read much," the goose said.

"Would you mind if I gave you some advice?" I asked.

"Not at all," the goose said.

"Appearing in my room and being an English-speaking, six-foot-tall magic goose is all very well and good," I said. "And you did that part very nicely."

"Thank you," said the goose.

"But you need to have some sort of a plan," I said. "There ought to be a magic activity. It's not enough just to come down to the kitchen and fix cornflakes."

"Cornflakes soup," said the goose.

"Whatever."

4
A Magic Activity

"I'd welcome any suggestions," the goose said.

"Let me think a minute," I said. "You can fly, I suppose."

"I'm a goose."

"How about this? I get on your back, and you take me flying?"

"It sounds unsafe," the goose said.

"I hang on to your feathers," I said.

"That might hurt," said the goose.

"I take the belt from my bathrobe, tie it

around your neck, and hold on to that, all right?"

"That would work," said the goose.

"So you'll take me flying?" I asked.

"For how long?"

"For a while! What does it matter? Do you have other kids to visit tonight?"

"No."

"Do you have to be back in Magic Goose Land, or wherever you come from, at some special time?"

"No."

"So let's go already! By the way, where *do* you come from?"

"Magic Goose Land."

I led the goose out into the backyard.

"Nice yard," the goose said.

"Thanks," I said. I took the belt from my bathrobe and tied it around the goose's neck.

"Not too tight," the goose said.

"Relax. I know what I'm doing," I said. "How does that feel?"

"It feels okay," the goose said. "What if it comes undone when we're flying?"

"I did a square knot with a double fisherman's bend," I said. "There's a whole section with illustrations about knots in *The Haphazard House Junior Dictionary for Little Scholars*. This won't come undone."

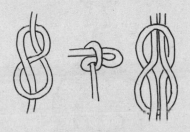

I climbed onto the goose's back and took a tight hold of the bathrobe belt.

"Let's go," I said.

"It feels funny with you on my back," the goose said.

"Just fly. You'll get used to it."

The goose spread its wings. I held tight.

This is exciting! I thought.

"I can't do it," said the goose.

"What do you mean, you can't do it?" I asked.

"All of a sudden, I sort of forgot how to get off the ground," the goose said. "It doesn't feel right, with you sitting on my back."

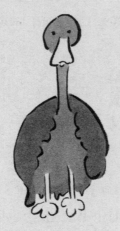

"Just fly," I said. "Don't think about me. Just fly the way you usually do."

The goose flapped its wings. I felt a great rush of air. I held on extra tight. The goose flapped faster.

"We're not moving," I said.

"We're not?" the goose asked.

"We're not moving an inch," I said.

"I can't understand it," the goose said. "Why can't I get off the ground?"

"It's because of the extra weight," I said. "You'll have to do a running takeoff."

I climbed down off the goose's back and led the goose by the bathrobe belt. I led him to the far end of the backyard.

"Now, what you have to do is start running and flapping," I said.

"What will that do?" the goose asked.

"We'll build up speed, running along the ground, and the movement of air under your wings will help us take off."

"You think so?" the goose asked.

"I'm sure of it. That's how airplanes take off."

"How do you know so much?" the goose asked.

aviation *ay-vee-ay-shun*\\: the operation of heavier-than-air aircraft

"I read about it," I said. "Now, let's try it."

The goose began to run. Its webbed feet slapped against the ground.

"Flap your wings! Flap your wings!" I shouted.

"Too many things to think about!" the goose shouted.

We got to the end of the yard.

"I have to rest for a minute," the goose said. "I'm getting all confused."

I waited while the goose stood quietly, composing himself.

"Ready to try again?" I asked him.

"Yes."

"Let's go back to the other end of the yard and try again," I said. "This time, start flapping before you start running."

"Why not just turn around and run the other way?" the goose asked.

"Because we have to run into the wind. It will help us take off."

"You read about that, too?" the goose asked.

> **aeronautics** *ay-ro-naw-tiks*\\: the art or science of flight

> **takeoff** *tayk-awf*\\: a rise or leap from a surface in making a jump or flight or an ascent in an aircraft or in the launching of a rocket

> **windward:** being in or facing the direction from which the wind is blowing — compare LEEWARD

"Yes," I said.

The goose and I went back to the far end

of the backyard. I climbed onto the goose's
back.

"This time, I will tell you what to do, and
you will do it," I said. "Ready?"

"Ready!" said the goose.

"Flap!" I shouted.

The goose flapped.

"Flap faster!"

The goose flapped faster.

"Flap very fast!"

"I'm flapping as fast as I can!" the goose shouted.

The goose was flapping its wings very fast. I felt the rush of air, and dust and bits of grass were whirling around and hitting me in the face.

"Now, run!" I shouted.

The goose ran.

"Run faster! Flap harder!"

I heard the goose's webbed feet slapping against the backyard grass. Then I felt the goose bob upward. The sound of the feet had changed from slapping to scratching. The goose was running on tiptoe. Another bob, and I could not hear the feet at all. Over the goose's head I saw the backyard fence drop down and pass underneath us.

"We're flying!"

5
Night
Flying

"This is definitely neat," I said.

"It feels funny flying with someone on my back," the goose said.

We were high above the neighborhood. I could see my house and my street. Things looked different from high in the air. It looked like a toy neighborhood. The houses were like toy houses, and the cars were like toy cars. The streetlights were like little flashlights, blinking through the trees.

"Neat!" I said. "Neat, neat."

"I get to see stuff like this all the time,"

the goose said. "I guess it is kind of neat, now that you mention it."

"Let's fly over my school!" I said.

"Which way is it?" the goose asked.

"Hang a left."

The goose flew over the same streets I walked on going to school every day. There was the school building, with all its lights out.

"There it is! That's my school!" I said.

"Nice school," the goose said.

"Fly around it!"

The goose flew slowly around the school.

"This would be great if we could do it on a school morning," I said. "You could fly me to school. The kids would go wild when they saw me arrive on a magic goose."

"I suppose it would sort of blow their

minds," the goose said. "You want to fly around the school again?"

"No, let's go up high!"

"Sure you won't be scared?" the goose asked. "I can go pretty high."

"I am not scared, and I will not be scared," I said. "Go as high as you can."

The goose flew in big circles, rising higher and higher. The streets and houses got smaller and smaller and soon were lost in the clouds. We were surrounded by stars and the night sky.

"Look how big the moon seems!" I said.

"It *is* big," the goose said.

"Is this as high as you have ever gone?" I asked.

"I have never been this high," the goose said. "I feel a little bit dizzy."

"It's cold up here," I said. "But it's neat."

"I'm scared," the goose said. "I'm going to fly lower down."

"I'm not scared," I said. "But if you want to go lower down, it's all right with me." I was *not* scared, not really, but I was feeling a little dizzy myself. I did not tell the goose.

"Thank you," said the goose.

The goose slowly descended through the clouds, and we saw the lights and houses again.

"Look at the big buildings downtown!" I said. "Can we fly over there?"

"Why not?" said the goose.

The tall buildings were mostly dark. The goose flew between them. With the buildings on both sides, it was like flying through canyons, and I could feel how fast the goose was going.

"Yaaay! This is great!" I shouted.

"Watch this," the goose said. "I can do loops!"

The goose flew loops and loop-the-loops between the tall buildings.

I held on tight.

"Do it again!" I shouted.

"Let's go up to the tops of the buildings," the goose said.

"Okay."

The goose flew up until we were as high as the buildings. I noticed that it was very quiet. When I had been downtown before, it had always been during the day, and there had been lots of noise from buses and cars, engines and horns. Now, with the buildings mostly dark, there wasn't a sound.

Then, I heard something. It was a sweet sound. "Do you hear that?" I asked the goose.

"That music?" the goose asked.

"Yes!" I said. "Where is it coming from?"

In one of the dark buildings, near the very top, there was a light in a window. The goose flew near to the window, and I could

see a man sitting in a chair, with his feet on a desk, playing a clarinet.

"He's good," the goose said. "He must be someone who works late at night. I assume he's taking a break to play some music. Maybe this is his nighttime lunch hour."

"Let's listen," I said.

The goose landed on the roof of the building just across the street from the one in which the man was playing the clarinet. I climbed off the goose's back, and we listened to the music. The man in the building went into a fast tune, and the goose and I began to tap our feet.

The moon cast a beautiful light on the deserted downtown, the clarinet music drifted between the skyscrapers, and I danced with the goose until the man in the window put his clarinet away and went back to working at the computer on his desk.

6
Magic Goose Land

"Let's fly out into the country," I said.

"Suits me," said the goose. "Climb on my back."

The goose, with me on his back, hurled himself from the roof of the tall building, rose into the sky, and soon the lights of the city were far behind us.

"It's dark out here," the goose said. "There's not much to see."

"There's a river," I said. "You can see it shining in the moonlight."

"So you can," the goose said. "Sort of pretty, isn't it?"

"What's that smell?" I asked. I was smelling something very strong.

"You don't know what that smell is?" the goose asked.

"No," I said. "It's pretty powerful. What is it?"

"I'll show you," the goose said.

The goose flew straight for the smell. It got stronger as we got closer.

"Phew! What is it?" I asked.

"You'll see," said the goose.

We landed in a big open place. There were hundreds and hundreds of geese standing around. It didn't smell very nice.

"What is this place?" I asked.

"Magic Goose Land!" the goose said.

I looked around. The place was surrounded by a high fence. The hundreds and hundreds of geese were white, not gray like my goose.

"This is Magic Goose Land?" I asked.

"Neat, isn't it?" the goose said.

"These geese are all magic?"

"Every one of them," the goose said.

"They aren't paying any attention to us," I said.

"They're just being polite," the goose said. "It would be rude to make a fuss."

"Do you know these geese?" I asked.

The goose looked around. "I don't see anyone I actually know," it said.

"Are you sure this is Magic Goose Land?" I asked.

"It does seem different somehow," the goose said. "On the other hand, what else could it be?"

"I think this is a goose farm," I said.

"A goose farm? What's a goose farm?"

goose *gooss*\\ **1:** any of numerous large waterfowl (family Anatidae) that are intermediate between the swans and ducks **2:** SIMPLETON, DOLT

farm *farm*\\: a plot of land devoted to agricultural purposes, the raising of animals and *esp.* domestic livestock

"A goose farm is where they keep lots of geese."

"So? How is that different from Magic Goose Land?" the goose asked.

"These geese aren't magic," I said.

"They aren't?" asked the goose. "So what are they doing standing around here?"

"These geese," I said, "are going to be eaten."

"You're kidding!"

"I'm afraid not," I said.

"No, really. Be serious," said the goose.

"They're going to be eaten? Who would do such a thing?"

"People," I said. "People eat geese."

The goose looked at me.

"Oh, not me! Not me! I have never eaten a goose! I don't think anyone in my family has ever eaten a goose."

"This is a joke in doubtful taste," the goose said.

"It is not a joke," I said.

"In that case, I think we should leave," the goose said.

"Yes," I said.

"Just a moment," the goose said. He walked over to where a bunch of geese were standing around, not doing anything.

"Excuse me," he said. "I don't wish to alarm you, but I am informed that you are going to be eaten."

"Honk," said the farmyard goose.

"No, I really mean it," my goose said. "I

know it sounds silly, but you should really think about getting out of here."

"Honk."

"My friend and I would be happy to help you escape," my goose said.

"What are you, some kind of magic goose?" the farm goose replied.

"Well, as a matter of fact . . ."

"Is that how you know so much?" the farm goose honked.

"Yes."

"Well, I'll tell you something, Mr. Magic Goose. You and your friend are crazy as bats. Who would eat a goose? It's ridiculous! You might as well say that someone would eat a cow!"

The goose came back to where I was standing.

"Were you really serious when you said these geese are going to be eaten?" he asked.

"Yes, and have their feathers made into pillows," I said.

"Pillows?"

> **goose down** *goossdoun*\: the soft feathers of a goose, used in making pillows and comforters

"That's right," I said.

"Very funny," the goose said. "No wonder that other goose thought I was an idiot. You have a warped sense of humor."

"I'm serious," I said.

"Right," said the goose. "Let's go now."

7
Lost
Goose

"I promise, those geese are going to be eaten," I said to the goose as we flew away. "I wasn't playing a joke on you."

"You'll say anything for a laugh, right?" the goose said. "I suppose I'd think it was funny, too, but I've got a problem that's bothering me."

"You do? What is it?" I asked.

"I don't like to bother you," said the goose.

"You won't be bothering me," I said. "We're friends."

"We are?"

"Of course we are. What is your problem?"

"You don't happen to know how to get to Magic Goose Land, by any chance?" the goose asked me.

"You don't know?"

"I just wondered if you knew," the goose said.

"You thought the goose farm was Magic Goose Land," I said.

"It was a mistake anybody could have made."

"Do you remember how you got here?" I asked.

"Not precisely," the goose said.

"You just turned up in my room, and you have no idea how you got there?"

"Yes," the goose said.

"What do you remember about coming here?" I asked.

"Not much," the goose said. "I sort of tend to live in the present moment. Geese are like that."

"So, you're completely lost."

"I would say that I am completely lost," the goose said.

"I thought geese were very good at traveling long distances and finding their way."

"There are leaders and there are followers. I never paid much attention."

"We could look for it on a map," I said.

"What's a map?"

> **map** *map***:** a representation usually on a flat surface of the whole or a part of an area

> **cartography** *kar-tog-ruh-fee***:** the science or art of making maps

"But I'm pretty sure it won't be on a map," I said. "This has to do with magic, and maps usually don't."

"Well, please don't worry about it," the goose said. "I will be fine."

"We need to ask somebody," I said.

"Could we ask your mother and father?" the goose asked.

"We could," I said. "But I don't think they'd know about Magic Goose Land. Besides, I'd have to explain why I was flying around with you when I was supposed to be asleep. I think we should ask somebody else."

"Who?"

"I think we should ask Nathaniel Inkblotter, author of *Seymour and the Magic Pudding,* my favorite book! He knows about magic things that turn up at night!"

"Fine. Let's ask him," the goose said. "Do you know where he lives?"

"I know how to find out," I said. "Let's look for a telephone booth. We can look him up in the directory."

directory \duh-rek-tuh-ree\: an alphabetical or classified list (as of names and addresses): a phone book

8
Nathaniel
Inkblotter

It turned out that Nathaniel Inkblotter, the famous author, lived in the Crummy Creek Trailer Park. The goose and I flew there. We found Mr. Inkblotter's trailer. It had a rusted-up old car outside with a bumper sticker that said *I'd rather be writing*. All the windows of the trailer were dark.

"I forgot it was so late at night," I said. "He must be sleeping. Maybe we should come back in the morning."

"You forget I am a magic goose," the

goose said. "I will appear in his bedroom. It's something I do well."

"Good idea," I said. "And he'll probably like it. After all, he writes about stuff like that."

I helped the goose clamber into an open window. He was heavy, and it was hard work. I had to sort of stuff him in. Then I

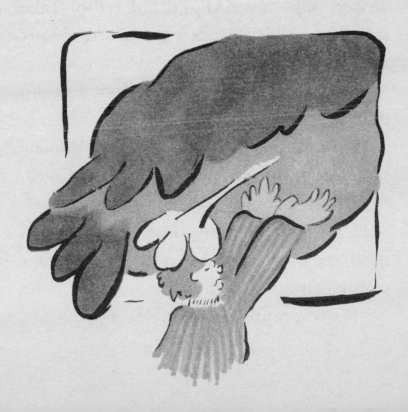

waited outside Nathaniel Inkblotter's trailer.

I heard a couple of thumps and crashes. Apparently the goose had bumped into things in the dark. Then, I heard nothing for a while.

A light came on, and I heard a blood-freezing scream.

"Oh, no! Bandits! Spare me! Don't take my life! Take my money! Take my type-writer! Take my AM and FM radio! Take my electric waffle iron! But do not hurt me!"

That was Nathaniel Inkblotter. I could hear the goose talking.

"I am not a bandit. I am a magic goose."

"Eeek! Evil spirits! Oh, no! Nooooo!" Nathaniel Inkblotter wailed.

"I am not evil," the goose said. "I am an ordinary magic goose, and I do not want your electric waffle iron."

"I am going into this closet," I heard

Nathaniel Inkblotter say. "And I am not coming out until you are gone. Depart, evil goose! I defy your dreadful powers!"

I heard a door slam.

"Mr. Inkblotter," the goose said. "Please come out. My friend and I just want to ask your advice."

"You have a fiend with you?" Nathaniel Inkblotter said from inside the closet. "I want you to know that I have in this closet a special fiend-bashing tennis racquet. If I whap you with this, you evil creature, it will all be over for you and your fiend, too, so avaunt, get it?"

avaunt \ah-vawnt\: away, hence, get lost!

The goose appeared at the door of the trailer.

"Seymour, maybe you could come in

55

here and talk to Mr. Inkblotter. I think he dislikes me."

I went inside the trailer. I made my way to the closet door and knocked.

"Mr. Inkblotter?"

"Go away, monster!" Nathaniel Inkblotter said.

"I am not a monster. I am a boy. I have a magic goose with me. We are sorry to wake you up like this. I read your book, *Seymour and the Magic Pudding*."

"You read my book?"

"Yes. It is my favorite book," I said.

"Oh. Really?" Nathaniel Inkblotter opened the closet door a tiny bit. "It's your favorite book?"

"I must have read it fifteen times."

He opened the door a little more.

"And you and that goose aren't monsters?"

"No we are not," I said. "Just a boy and a magic goose."

Nathaniel Inkblotter stepped out of the closet. He was wearing pink pajamas and carrying the tennis racquet.

"You promise?"

"Word of honor," I said.

"You like my book, do you?"

"I just love it," I said.

Nathaniel Inkblotter put the tennis racquet into the closet.

"So, what can I do for you?" he asked.

9
Home
Again

Nathaniel Inkblotter and the goose decided to go looking for Magic Goose Land together. When he got over being terrified, Nathaniel Inkblotter was very happy to meet a magic goose. He also liked that my name was Seymour, like the boy in his book. We sat in the little kitchen of his trailer and had grape juice in glasses with cartoons on them.

"When will we start looking for Magic Goose Land?" the goose asked.

"We will leave at once," Nathaniel Inkblotter said. "We will go in my car, we will pull the trailer with us, and we will find Magic Goose Land if it takes until next October!"

We had one more glass of grape juice, and Nathaniel Inkblotter gave me an autographed copy of his new book, *Seymour and the Talking Electric Waffle Iron*. Then they drove me home.

When we got to my house, the goose came with me to the kitchen door. Nathaniel Inkblotter waited in the car.

"I will be going now," the goose said. "Good-bye."

"Will you come back?"

"Maybe," said the goose, "Maybe not. Here. You can have this."

The goose gave me something.

"What is this?"

"A present."

It was a green plastic pickle.

"Blow it," said the goose.

I blew it. It made a sound like the wind whistling through the goose's wings.

"It's a whistle!" I said.

"Yep."

"Is it magic?" I asked.

"Well, you got it from a magic goose."

"That's true."

"I'm going," said the goose. "Thanks for the cornflakes soup."

"You're welcome. Thanks for the goose-back ride and the pickle whistle. I hope you and Nathaniel Inkblotter find Magic Goose Land."

"Good-bye, kid."

"Good-bye, goose."

I went into the house. I washed the dishes we had used when we made cornflakes soup. I went back to my room. I looked at the pickle whistle.

A magic goose gave me this, I thought.

Nathaniel Inkblotter might write a story, I thought. He might call it *Seymour, the Magic Goose, and the Green Plastic Pickle Whistle.*

Then I went to sleep.

LITTLE 🍎 APPLE®

Here are some of our favorite Little Apples.

There are fun times ahead with kids just like you in Little Apple books! Once you take a bite out of a Little Apple—you'll want to read more!

Reading Excitement for Kids with BIG Appetites!

☐ NA45899-X **Amber Brown Is Not a Crayon**
Paula Danziger $2.99

☐ NA93425-2 **Amber Brown Goes Fourth**
Paula Danziger $2.99

☐ NA50207-7 **You Can't Eat Your Chicken Pox, Amber Brown**
Paula Danziger $2.99

☐ NA42833-0 **Catwings** Ursula K. LeGuin $2.95

☐ NA42832-2 **Catwings Return** Ursula K. LeGuin $3.50

☐ NA41821-1 **Class Clown** Johanna Hurwitz $2.99

☐ NA42400-9 **Five True Horse Stories**
Margaret Davidson $2.99

☐ NA43868-9 **The Haunting of Grade Three**
Grace Maccarone $2.99

☐ NA40966-2 **Rent a Third Grader** B.B. Hiller $2.99

☐ NA41944-7 **The Return of the Third Grade Ghost Hunters**
Grace Maccarone $2.99

☐ NA42031-3 **Teacher's Pet** Johanna Hurwitz $3.50

Available wherever you buy books...or use the coupon below.

- -

SCHOLASTIC INC., P.O. Box 7502, 2931 East McCarty Street, Jefferson City, MO 65102

Please send me the books I have checked above. I am enclosing $ _____ (please add $2.00 to cover shipping and handling). Send check or money order—no cash or C.O.D.s please.

Name_____

Address_____

City_____State/Zip_____

Please allow four to six weeks for delivery. Offer good in the U.S.A. only. Sorry, mail orders are not available to residents of Canada. Prices subject to change.   LA996

The Adventures of THE BAILEY SCHOOL KIDS ®

Creepy, weird, wacky and funny things happen to the Bailey School Kids!™ Collect and read them all!

Available wherever you buy books, or use this order form

Scholastic Inc., P.O. Box 7502, Jefferson City, MO 65102

Please send me the books I have checked above. I am enclosing $_____ (please add $2.00 to cover shipping and handling). Send check or money order — no cash or C.O.D.s please.

Name _____

Address _____

City _____ State/Zip _____

Please allow four to six weeks for delivery. Offer good in the U.S. only. Sorry, mail orders are not available to residents of Canada. Prices subject to change.   BSK397

Pony Pals®

Be a Pony Pal!

Anna, Pam, and Lulu want you to join them on adventures with their favorite ponies!

Order now and you get a free pony portrait bookmark and two collecting cards in all the books—for you *and* your pony pal!

❑ BBC48583-0	#1	I Want a Pony	$2.99
❑ BBC48584-9	#2	A Pony for Keeps	$2.99
❑ BBC48585-7	#3	A Pony in Trouble	$2.99
❑ BBC48586-5	#4	Give Me Back My Pony	$2.99
❑ BBC25244-5	#5	Pony to the Rescue	$2.99
❑ BBC25245-3	#6	Too Many Ponies	$2.99
❑ BBC54338-5	#7	Runaway Pony	$2.99
❑ BBC54339-3	#8	Good-bye Pony	$2.99
❑ BBC62974-3	#9	The Wild Pony	$2.99
❑ BBC62975-1	#10	Don't Hurt My Pony	$2.99
❑ BBC86597-8	#11	Circus Pony	$2.99
❑ BBC86598-6	#12	Keep Out, Pony!	$2.99
❑ BBC86600-1	#13	The Girl Who Hated Ponies	$2.99
❑ BBC86601-X	#14	Pony-Sitters	$3.50
❑ BBC86632-X	#15	The Blind Pony	$3.50
❑ BBC37459-1	#16	The Missing Pony Pal	$3.50
❑ BBC74210-8		Pony Pals Super Special #1: The Baby Pony	$5.99
❑ BBC86631-1		Pony Pals Super Special #2: The Lives of our Ponies	$5.99
❑ BBC37461-3		Pony Pals Super Special #3: The Ghost Pony	$5.99

Available wherever you buy books, or use this order form.

Send orders to Scholastic Inc., P.O. Box 7500, Jefferson City, MO 65102

Please send me the books I have checked above. I am enclosing $_____ (please add $2.00 to cover shipping and handling). Send check or money order — no cash or C.O.D.s please.

Please allow four to six weeks for delivery. Offer good in the U.S.A. only. Sorry, mail orders are not available to residents in Canada. Prices subject to change.

Name_____ Birthdate ___/___/___
    First   Last   M   D   Y

Address_____

City_____ State_____ Zip_____

Telephone (_____)_____ ❑ Boy ❑ Girl

Where did you buy this book? ❑ Bookstore ❑ Book Fair ❑ Book Club ❑ Other

PP497